Henry
and the
Kite
Dragon

BRUCE EDWARD HALL

Illustrated by WILLIAM LOW

PHILOMEL BOOKS
NEW YORK

This story is based on true events. When my father was a little boy in Chinatown in the 1920s, there was an old man named Mr. Chin who lived in his building. He made wonderful kites and let a few lucky kids help fly them. Henry's adventure is inspired by him.   —Bruce Edward Hall

For Hana   —BEH

For Timothy and Jennifer   —WL

Text copyright © 2004 by Bruce Edward Hall. Illustrations copyright © 2004 by William Low.
All rights reserved. This book, or parts thereof, may not be reproduced in any form without permission in writing from the publisher, PHILOMEL BOOKS, a division of Penguin Young Readers Group, 345 Hudson Street, New York, NY 10014. Philomel Books, Reg. U.S. Pat. & Tm. Off. The scanning, uploading and distribution of this book via the Internet or via any other means without the permission of the publisher is illegal and punishable by law. Please purchase only authorized electronic editions, and do not participate in or encourage electronic piracy of copyrighted materials. Your support of the author's rights is appreciated. Published simultaneously in Canada. Manufactured in China by South China Printing Co. Ltd.   Designed by Semadar Megged.   Text set in 16-point Closter.
Library of Congress Cataloging-in-Publication Data
Hall, Bruce Edward.   Henry and the kite dragon / by Bruce Edward Hall ; illustrated by William Low.   p. cm.   Summary: In New York City in the 1920s, the children from Chinatown go after the children from Little Italy for throwing rocks at the beautiful kites Grandfather Chin makes, not realizing that they have a reason for doing so.   [1. Kites—Fiction. 2. Prejudices—Fiction. 3. Chinese Americans—Fiction. 4. Italian Americans—Fiction. 5. Chinatown (New York, N.Y.)—History—20th century—Fiction. 6. New York (N.Y.)—History—20th century—Fiction.] I. Low, William, ill. II. Title.   PZ7.H441136 He 2004   [E]—dc22   2003016381   ISBN 0-399-23727-5
10 9 8 7 6 5 4 3 2 1
First Impression

My name is Henry Chu. I am eight years old.

I live in a place called Chinatown in New York City. Chinatown is very small—pretty much just three tiny streets, all narrow and crooked, like a village in China would be.

Doyers Street is the littlest and crookedest street in Chinatown. It has a place to buy tasty little dumplings to have with our tea. I like the ones with shrimp. My friend Thelma Fung likes the ones with sweet roast pork. Mott Street is where my family lives. Our building is the tallest of all. From one side you can see all the way down to Pell Street, and on the other, you can look right down into the next neighborhood. It's called Little Italy.

In Chinatown, New York, there are lots of things to do for fun. You can buy sweet, pickled onions from Mrs. Lee's stand for two cents each.

You can watch Mr. Eng sort mail at the littlest post office in New York. (It's only eight feet wide!)

But my favorite thing to do in Chinatown, more favorite than anything, is—fly kites!

And on the top floor of my building lives a man who makes the best kites of all, the best kites in the whole wide world. His name is Mr. Chin, but we kids call him Grandfather. It's a sign of respect for his age.

When he was a kid in China, everyone made kites. But his kites were the biggest and the prettiest, flew the highest, and always won first prize in all the contests. He is little and old now, and always wears a sweater with holes and worn-out brown slippers. But he still likes to climb the stairs to the roof to fly one of his famous kites shaped like a butterfly, or a caterpillar, or his specialty, a big, beautiful dragon.

My friend Thelma Fung and I get to help Grandfather Chin make them.

One time we made a butterfly from broken-up packing crates. The body was made from cardboard. We used the big pot of rice paste that Grandfather Chin boiled on the stove to stick on sheets of newspaper to make wings.

Grandfather Chin painted on bright orange stripes and deep purple spots and glued on glittery gold foil and blue polka dots.

Thelma Fung and I thought it was the best, most wonderful butterfly we'd ever seen!

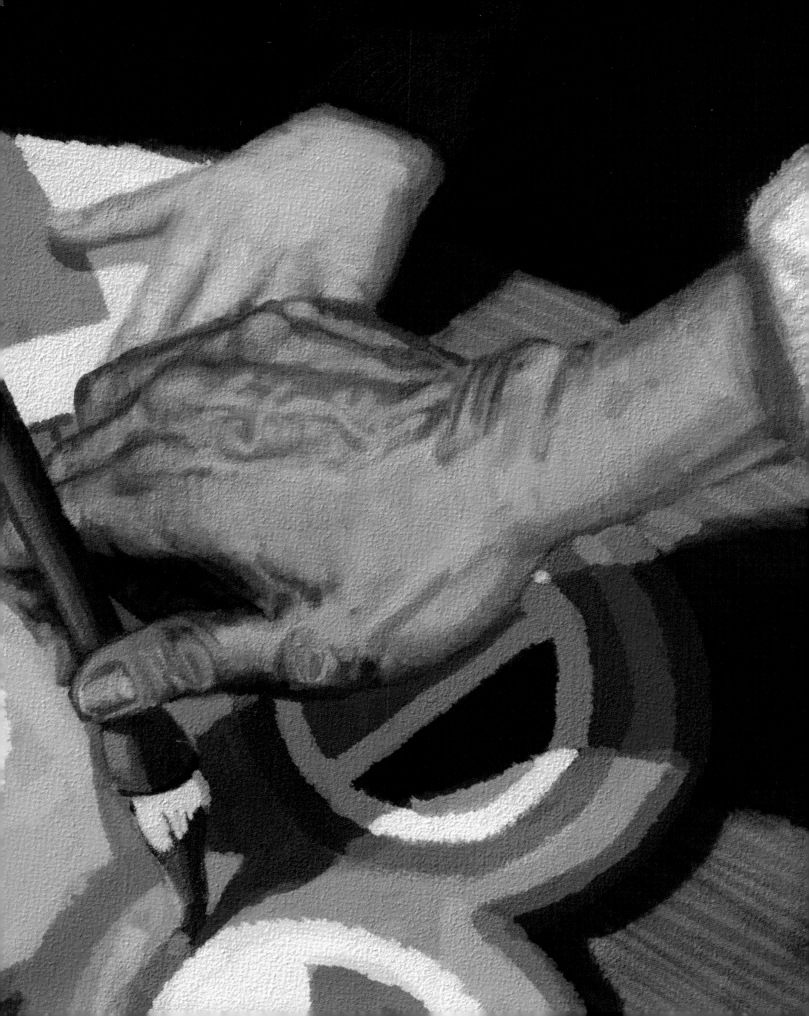

Up on the roof, it was a perfect kite-flying day. A brisk breeze, not too cold, and sunshine broken up by clouds skipping across the sky.

But Grandfather Chin was not only a great kite maker, he was a great kite flier. Slowly, he let the butterfly rise up—and out—and over—until it caught the wind and just took off!

He made the butterfly do swoops. He made it do swirls. He made it do loop-the-loops and reverse curls.

Our butterfly seemed alive!

A pigeon flew by, and in a flash, Grandfather Chin made the kite chase the little bird, as if our big, beautiful butterfly were going to eat him up! The pigeon flew away as fast as his wings could carry him. Our new friend, the butterfly, sailed over the building behind us and paused over the park in Little Italy, a block away.

But then, something happened.

A kid named Tony Guglione (that's goog-lee-ON-ee) saw our kite.

WHIZZ! A rock flew past our beautiful butterfly. WHOOSH! ZING! Two more went by, one of them just nicking the wing. Then—

SMASH! CRASH! RIP! A whole hail of rocks and pebbles tore through the butterfly's wings. Trembling as if in pain, the wonderful butterfly sank slowly to the ground, right into the park.

Tony and his friends tore the kite to bits. They ripped it and stomped on it and shook their fists.

Tony always made trouble for us Chinese kids.

And that's why we never went into the park when he and his friends were there.

Grandfather Chin just watched, never uttering a word.
Finally, he turned to Thelma Fung and me and said,
"Well, we'll just have to go and make another one."

The next day, we three made a caterpillar kite. It was long and sleek, painted bright yellow with red spots, and had a face that made it look like it was surprised to be flying in the clouds at the end of a string.

The sky was overcast, and there was the smell of rain in the air. Grandfather Chin made the caterpillar chase its own tail. He made it wave like the ocean. He made it squiggle and spiral.

This time, two pigeons appeared, and Grandfather Chin sent the giant caterpillar racing after them. They were terrified, and shot away from the kite.

But then, it happened again.

WHOOSH! went a rock. ZING! went another. Then Tony Guglione tied a long string to a stone and threw it right over the caterpillar's string, like a lasso. Now Tony and his friends reeled in our beautiful caterpillar, and once again our kite was stomped to pieces.

"Let's go beat them up!" I shouted. "Let's get all our friends and go down there and fight them!"

But Grandfather Chin just shook his head. "I have a better idea. But yes, get all of your friends."

Oh, good, I thought. Tony and his friends will leave us alone once and for all!

Soon, all our Chinatown buddies were climbing the stairs to Grandfather Chin's apartment—Everett Sing, Frances Eng, Walter Hom, Constance Ling, and others. But when we got there, we couldn't believe our eyes! Pots of paste boiled on the stove. Old wooden crates were everywhere, and so were stacks of colorful rice paper. "Come on! Come on!" Grandfather Chin said. "We have a kite to make!"

Make a kite? Now? But what could we do? After all, it was Grandfather Chin. So we rolled up our sleeves.

That day's kite was a dragon. It was huge, stretching from one end of the kitchen to the other and back again—who knew how long it was! It was covered in dazzling red rice paper and had two six-foot-long streamers for a tail. They were made of gold rice paper.

At last the dragon kite was ready. It was so long, it took all of us to carry it to the roof.

"This kite is so big and so beautiful that they wouldn't dare throw rocks at it!" Grandfather Chin said. "Everyone respects dragons! You'll see!"

There was another pigeon flying around, just one lonely bird, all by himself. We wanted the kite to chase it, but before we could even get the dragon in the air, Tony and his friends started throwing rocks again.

That's when I got really mad.

"Come on!" I shouted, and led my friends down eight flights of stairs and out onto the street, leaving Grandfather Chin and the giant dragon kite on the roof, alone.

"Wait!" Grandfather Chin called after us. "Where are you going?"

But we kids just kept on walking, right down Mott Street, making a right turn at the Catholic church, and marching one short block into the park where Tony and his friends were waiting. Chinese kids never went into the park when Tony Guglione was there.

But we did that day.

At first, Tony and his friends just stood with their mouths open. There was silence for a minute. Then Tony spoke.

"Ching chong, Chinamen!" Tony Guglione jeered.

"Stop it!" I yelled. "Tony—Goo-goo eyes!"

He was stunned. "Get out of our park!" he finally sputtered.

"No, you get out!"

"No, you!"

"YOU!"

"We were here first!"

We were all lined up, breathing hard, ready to start swinging, when all of a sudden, the sky went dark.

A big splash of color seemed to stretch across the entire sky. It was so big, it blotted out the sun like a giant cloud.

Grandfather Chin had launched the dragon by himself.

For a moment, everyone in the park was quiet as the gigantic creature hung in the air above our building—and then it started to dance.

It made a slow curve. Everyone said, "Oooh!"

It made a majestic swing. Everybody said, "Ahhh!"

And then that pigeon flew by. The dragon darted after the little bird, as if it were going to swallow it up in one bite.

"Stop it! Stop it!" Tony screamed. "That's my pigeon!"

"Huh?" we all said. "*Your* pigeon? What are you talking about?"

That's when I began to understand. In Little Italy they kept pet pigeons—homing pigeons—in cages on their roofs. He told me that homing pigeons are specially trained to always come home. He told me how our kites scared the little birds, and sometimes they flew away and never came back.

"And that pigeon is my favorite! Make that dragon leave my pigeon alone!"

Then great big Tony Guglione actually started to cry.

I didn't know what to say. Thelma Fung didn't know what to say. Everett Sing, Frances Eng, and Constance Ling didn't know what to say. We all just stood there, too surprised to move.

And then I got an idea. "Grandfather Chin! Stop!" I shouted up to the rooftop.

Frances Eng, Walter Hom, and Constance Ling joined in.

Then even Tony and his friends started shouting, "Grandfather—Grandfather—(what's his name?) —Grandfather Chin! Stop!"

All at once we started running up the hill to Mott Street, the Chinese kids, Tony Guglione and his friends—everybody—running and shouting, "Grandfather Chin! Stop! Stop!"

We ran right up to our building, dashed through the door and up the stairs, still shouting, "Grandfather Chin! Stop! Stop!" By the time we got there, we were all out of breath.

"Grandfather . . . stop . . . pigeon . . . pet . . . Tony's . . . please . . . oh."

Grandfather Chin just looked at me. Then he looked at Tony. Then he looked at my friends, and Tony's friends.

When we told him about Tony's pet bird, Grandfather immediately reeled in the big, beautiful dragon. My friends and I watched as the poor, frightened homing pigeon made a couple of big, graceful circles and flew off to a cage we could see on the roof of a building a couple of blocks away. Everyone let out a sigh of relief.

And then, for the first time, Tony took a good, hard look at our dragon kite. "Where did you buy it?"

We laughed and told him how we made kites out of packing crates and rice paper and how Grandfather Chin painted on the faces.

"I guess I'm sorry we threw rocks at them." He paused. "It was our pet birds we were worried about. . . ."

We Chinese kids were sorry, too, and we said so, one by one.

Then we had another idea. From that day on, the Chinese kids fly
kites in the mornings. The Italian kids fly their birds in the afternoons.
The really great thing about this is, now we can admire their birds,
and they can admire our kites.
And everybody can go to the park whenever they want.

The next kite Grandfather Chin made was a brand-new specialty. It was big. It was silvery. It was all shiny and shimmery. The kite he made was a giant pigeon. And now, when the kids in the park see it, all they say is
    "Ooooh!"